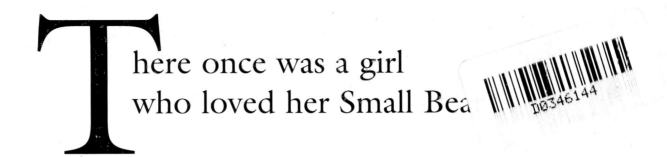

There once was a girl who loved her Small Bea

For Laura, David, Christopher and Rachel
M.W.

For the Fanning family
V.A.

First published 1996 by Walker Books Ltd, 87 Vauxhall Walk, London SE11 5HJ

This edition published 1997

Text © 1996 Martin Waddell. Illustrations © 1996 Virginia Austin

The right of Martin Waddell to be identified as the author of this work has been
asserted by him in accordance with the Copyright, Designs and Patents Act 1988.

4 6 8 10 9 7 5 3

Printed in Hong Kong

This book has been typeset in Galliard.

British Library Cataloguing in Publication Data: a catalogue record for this book is available from the British Library.

ISBN 0-7445-5263-X

Small Bear Lost

Written by
Martin Waddell

Illustrated by
Virginia Austin

WALKER BOOKS
AND SUBSIDIARIES
LONDON • BOSTON • SYDNEY

Small Bear went everywhere with the girl, but one day Small Bear went to sleep on the train. When he woke up the girl wasn't there. Small Bear was lost and alone. "I've got to find my way home," decided Small Bear.

Small Bear got off the train
at the next station.
He found a big map.
"That's where home is and
here's where I am. But there
isn't a train till a quarter to four,"
thought Small Bear.
He thought a bit more
and then...

"I'll catch the bus home," decided Small Bear. When the bus came Small Bear got on. Small Bear didn't pay any fare. He was such a *small* bear that he took up no room, or maybe small bears don't have to pay fares.

"I'll be home soon," thought Small Bear.

"There's my park," thought Small Bear
and he got off the bus at his stop.

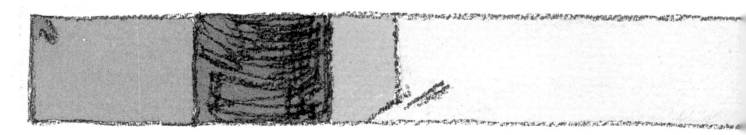

"I'm nearly home now," thought Small Bear,
setting off through the gates.

But he wasn't as near
to his house as he thought,
and small bears can't walk very
far for their small legs get sore.

"I can't walk any more,"
Small Bear decided and then…

Small Bear saw a bunch of
balloons caught up in the tree.
Small Bear liked balloons.
So he climbed up the tree and
grabbed the balloons
but…

The balloons lifted Small Bear off the high branch.

(Small bears don't weigh very much.)

Small Bear flew through the air, down,

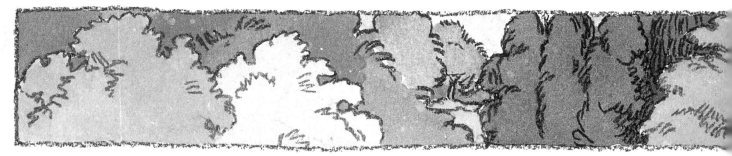

down, down, down and then…

OH, NO! The balloons caught
on the spikes on the wall.
"How do I get down?"
wondered Small Bear.

BANG! BANG! BANG!
The balloons burst
and Small Bear fell down.
He was all bumps and bruises
but…

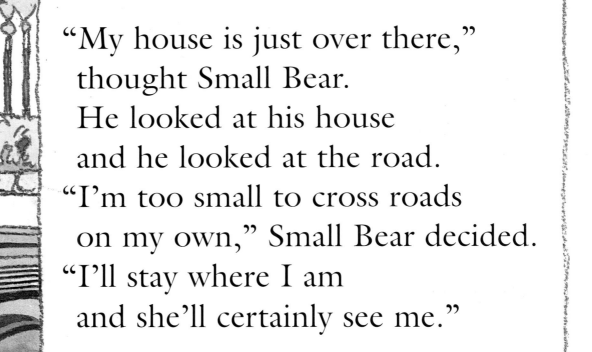

"My house is just over there,"
  thought Small Bear.
He looked at his house
  and he looked at the road.
"I'm too small to cross roads
  on my own," Small Bear decided.
"I'll stay where I am
  and she'll certainly see me."

Small Bear waited ...

and he waited …

and then the little girl and her mother

found Small Bear asleep by the gates.

"How did you get here,
Small Bear?" asked the girl.
"Where did I lose you?
How did you find your
way home?"

She never found out,
but that didn't bother
Small Bear…

Small Bear wasn't lost any more.